The Berenstain Bears'
DINOSAUR DIG

Jan & Mike Berenstain

A special kind of beast
lived very long ago.
Its different forms and names
are very good to know.

HARPER FESTIVAL
An Imprint of HarperCollinsPublishers

The Berenstain Bears' Dinosaur Dig
Copyright © 2012 by Berenstain Publishing, Inc.
For information address HarperCollins Children's Books, a division of HarperCollins Publishers, 195 Broadway, New York, NY 10007.
www.harpercollinschildrens.com
Library of Congress catalog card number: 2011927588
ISBN 978-0-06-207548-2
18 19 20   SCP   20 19 18 17 16 15 14
❖
First Edition

Brother and Sister Bear liked to read, and they went to the Bear Country Library quite often. They liked mysteries, adventures, sports stories, and lots of other books, too.

One day, Brother found a book about dinosaurs. He showed it to Sister and they looked at it together. It was very interesting.

Brother and Sister really liked all those dinosaurs. Learning about them was exciting. They liked their long, ferocious teeth. And they liked their long, ferocious names—like Tyrannosaurus, Stegosaurus, and Triceratops.

Stegosaurus had spikes on its tail. It could use them to whack big meat-eaters like Tyrannosaurus and Allosaurus, who had those long, ferocious teeth.

Al-o-SAW-rus

Triceratops had sharp horns on its head. It could use them to poke any other dinosaur who messed with it.

The best part was that they lived long, long ago, so you didn't have to worry about them getting you.

Mama and Papa were delighted that Brother and Sister had
this wonderful new interest—and Honey thought it was okay, too.
They all went to the Bearsonian Museum to see the dinosaur
skeletons. They were ginormous! Brother and Sister really liked
those dinosaur skeletons.

While they were at the museum, Professor Actual Factual saw them and stopped to say hello. He was the head of the museum and an old friend of the Bear family.

"I see you two cubs have been bitten by the dinosaur bug," he said, smiling.

"The dinosaur bug?" said Brother.

"What kind of bug is that?" asked Sister. She imagined a huge, prehistoric insect.

Professor Actual Factual laughed. "I just mean that you've caught an interest in dinosaurs and other prehistoric creatures. Once you've caught that bug, it's hard to get rid of. I know— I've got it, too!"

"In fact," said the professor, "would you like to see my latest dinosaur project?"

"Would we ever!" said Sister.

"You bet!" said Brother.

"Then just follow me," said the professor, leading them outside and to the rear of the museum.

They came to a big open pit in the ground. Mounds of earth were heaped up everywhere. Down in the pit, scientists were at work carefully digging away.

"What's all this?" said Papa, scratching his head.

"This is my latest dinosaur dig," explained the professor. "We have discovered a large group of dinosaur fossils right here behind the museum. We're digging them up so that we can study them."

"Wow!" said Brother. "Did you find a Tyrannosaurus?"

"Well, no," said the professor. "But we did find a Spinosaurus skeleton. Spinosaurus was a fierce dinosaur almost as big as Tyrannosaurus, and it had a huge fin on its back."

"Can we see it?" asked Sister.

"Of course," said the professor. "Right this way."

They all climbed down a ladder into the dinosaur dig.
"Now here's the Spinosaurus skeleton," said the professor. "It's the first one found in this area."
"Wowie!" said Brother. "It's humongous!"
"And over here," said the professor, "there are many other fossil reptiles."

As he led them through the dig, Brother and Sister imagined all the prehistoric creatures as they would have looked when they were alive.

They saw another fin-backed reptile, the Dimetrodon; a giant, long-necked Apatosaurus; a flying reptile, a pterodactyl; and a giant sea reptile, the Mosasaurus. It was bigger and more ferocious than any shark that ever swam the seas.

"Thank you for the tour, professor," said Mama, as they climbed out of the dig. "That was very interesting."

"Yeah!" said Sister and Brother together. "It was awesome!"

On the way out of the museum, they stopped in the museum shop to get more books and some dinosaur models and kits.

Back home, Brother and Sister soon had every inch of their tree house covered with model dinosaurs. There were dinosaurs and reptiles fighting on the stairs, eating on the table, sleeping on the sofa, and swimming in the bathtub. There were even some dinosaurs made of clay inside the refrigerator. Brother kept them there so they wouldn't get soft and squishy.

It seemed to Papa and Mama that dinosaurs were *everywhere*.

Before dinner, Papa headed for his favorite easy chair with the evening newspaper.

"Oh, Papa . . ." said Sister, as he started to sit.

"Yeow!" Papa yelled, jumping up.

"That's my setup of the Jurassic Age," Sister explained.

"Sister," said Papa, "I'm delighted that you and Brother have this wonderful new interest. But," he said as he carefully moved Sister's dinosaurs off his chair, "the Jurassic Age will just have to settle for the coffee table."

And with a sigh, he sat down to read his paper.